THE SUMMER OF DREAMS

The Story of a World's Fair Girl

THE SUMMER OF DREAMS

The Story of a World's Fair Girl

BY DOROTHY AND THOMAS HOOBLER

AND CAREY-GREENBERG ASSOCIATES

PICTURES BY RENÉE GRAEF

SILVER BURDETT PRESS

**Library of Congress Cataloging-
in-Publication Data**

Hoobler, Thomas.
The summer of dreams :
the story of a world's fair girl /
by Thomas and Dorothy Hoobler
and Carey-Greenberg Associates;
pictures by Renée Graef.
p.   cm.
Summary: In 1893 while working at the
Chicago World's Fair, a young Italian-American
girl meets two prominent women, Mrs. Potter Palmer
and Jane Addams, and learns about the achievements
of other women throughout history.
1. World's Columbian Exposition (1893 : Chicago,
Ill.)—Juvenile fiction.   [1. World's Columbian
Exposition (1893 : Chicago, Ill.)—Fiction.
2. Women—History—Fiction.   3. Italian Americans
—Fiction.   4. Chicago (Ill.)—Fiction.]
I. Hoobler, Dorothy.   II. Graef, Renée, ill.
III. Carey-Greenberg Associates.   IV. Title.
PZ7.H7623Su   1993
[Fic]—dc20   91-39101   CIP   AC

CONTENTS

CHAPTER ONE

Opening Day

TRUMPETS sounded a fanfare, and drums began to rumble. "Here they come!" shouted someone in the crowd. Cristina Ricci stood on her tiptoes to see. She and her mother had arrived very early to get a good place in front of the Administration Building.

By now, the whole plaza was filled with thousands of people. The crowd stretched along both sides of the huge pool in front of the building. Standing at the other end of the pool was a 65-foot-high statue of Liberty holding a dove. Down there, the first of the horse-drawn carriages appeared, bringing the great men and women that everyone wanted to see. Soldiers had to push the crowd back to make room for the carriages.

The Chicago Columbian Exposition was about to open at last! Chicago had planned this great fair to celebrate the 400th anniversary of Christopher Columbus's first voyage to America in 1492. On an empty swamp next to Lake Michigan, thousands of workers had built massive white buildings. But the fair had taken so long to complete that it didn't open until today—May 1, 1893.

The delay had only made people more eager to see the fair. Nations from all over the world, as well as each of the 45 states of the United States, had sent exhibits. It was going to be the biggest and best world's fair ever held.

Cristina jumped up and down with excitement when she saw Grover Cleveland, the president of the United States. He waved to the crowd as his open carriage passed up the long Court of Honor. Right behind him was a carriage that held the Duke and Duchess of Spain. And following them were dozens of other carriages bringing the vice president, governors, and members of royal families. This was going to be Chicago's proudest day.

The long line of carriages finally reached the gold-domed Administration Building. President Cleveland, a heavyset man with a bushy mustache, walked to the top of the steps. His guests followed, seating themselves on chairs behind him.

Cristina's eyes bugged out as she saw the lovely gowns and jewels worn by the princesses and duchesses. But most beautiful of all, Cristina thought, was Mrs. Potter Palmer, the richest woman in Chicago, who sat next to President Cleveland.

The president began to speak, but Cristina hardly heard what he said. She couldn't take her eyes off Mrs. Palmer. People said she lived in a house that looked like a castle. Her husband owned the biggest hotel in Chicago, the Palmer House.

Cristina's father had once taken her to see the hotel. An old friend of Papa's from Italy worked in its barber shop. When Cristina entered the shop, she looked down in amazement. The whole floor of the barber shop was lined with silver dollars! What must the inside of Mrs. Palmer's house be like?

The drums rolled again. The president had finished his speech. A man rushed forward, carrying a box with a wire attached to it. On top of the box was a gold switch. The president reached down and flipped it.

People began to shout in amazement. Cristina felt the stone steps beneath her feet tremble. She could hear rumbling noises in all the great white buildings that lined the Court of Honor. Fountains in the pool suddenly began to spray colored water. The windows of the buildings shone brightly as electric lights turned on inside.

Cristina knew what was happening, for Papa had explained it to her. The president had started the 127 huge electric generators that powered all the machinery, lights, and fountains at the Exposition. "They will make more power," Papa had said, "than a thousand locomotives, more than a hundred thousand horses." Most people of the time had only heard about electricity. The Exposition would show how important it could be.

Now the crowd broke up and people started off in all directions. There was so much to see. Hundreds of buildings held the products, art, inventions, and crafts of virtually every country in the world. The Manufactures Building alone was said to be large enough to hold the largest pyramid of Egypt with room to spare.

And that wasn't all. There was a long Midway that was like the world's biggest circus, with acrobats, dancers, and animal acts. Overshadowing the Midway was a huge iron wheel, 250 feet high. Nobody had ever seen anything like it before. It was scary to think that you could take a ride on it and go all the way to the top. Although the wheel's inventor, George Ferris, promised it would be safe, people still called it Ferris's Folly. Some of Cristina's friends said they were sure this Ferris Wheel would fall down. Even so, a lot of them wanted to be among the first to try it out.

Cristina knew that the lines would be long at each of the exhibits. But she didn't have to hurry, for she was probably the luckiest girl in Chicago. Both her Mamma and Papa were working at the fair, and when school ended she could come here every day!

Papa had a job with the Chicago Edison Company, which had built the electric generators. Mamma worked at the Children's Pavilion. Imagine! A whole building—just for children. It had been Mrs. Palmer's idea. The fair was so big that

people thought children would get tired walking around it. So Mrs. Palmer said, "We will
make the world's largest playhouse for them to
stay in while their parents see the Exposition."

The building contained a gym, a nursery for
babies, and a garden on the roof. To keep the
children occupied, women like Mamma had
been hired to teach them useful things. Cristina
thought this made the Pavilion a bit too much
like a school. But Mamma had said, "You come
with me and watch. Nobody will get bored, I
promise you."

A group of children was already waiting when
they arrived. Mamma worked in the kinder-
kitchen, showing children how to prepare
meals. Everybody in their neighborhood on the
South Side of Chicago said that Mamma was the
best cook they had ever known.

Mamma took off her hat and put on a big
white apron. "Cooking is fun!" she said. She
reached into a big barrel of flour and threw a
handful onto a stone-topped table.

"Come around, come around!" Mamma
called. The children gathered around the table.
Cristina helped to tie little aprons on each of
them. This was a good idea, for Mamma soon
had everyone dipping their hands in the flour

barrel and making small white mounds for themselves. Clouds of flour floated through the air.

Mamma showed them how to make a little well in the center of their flour mounds. "Just like a volcano, see?" she said. "Now the eggs."

Mamma took an egg in one hand. "Look how easy," she said, and cracked the egg with her fingers so that it broke neatly in two. The inside of the egg dropped smoothly into the center of the flour.

Cristina handed each child an egg. She smiled, for she knew what was going to happen now. At home, she had practiced a long time before she could do Mamma's trick with the egg. *Crack!* went the eggs. Pieces of shell and yolk spattered all over the table, and onto the children too. Some of the children laughed, but others looked at Mamma like they had done something wrong.

"Don't worry," said Mamma. "Pick out the pieces of shell, and stir the egg into the flour with your fingers. It all gets mixed together anyway." She walked around, helping each child and sometimes adding flour if the dough was too runny.

Pretty soon everyone had a big, sticky lump

of dough. "Now the fun begins," said Mamma. "Is everybody feeling strong?" The children nodded. "Then let's knead the dough." She pounded her palms down on the dough, and so did everybody else. Mamma showed them how to press their thumbs into the dough, pushing and turning it. "Keep it up till it turns silky and springy," she said.

This was actually the hard part, Cristina knew, but Mamma made it seem like fun. The room was filled with the sound of hands pounding dough against the table. When some children got tired, Mamma had them spread out more flour so the dough didn't stick to the table. But it took a lot of pounding to make the dough shine like silk.

"Is it done yet?" children kept asking.

"Not until it's alive," said Mamma. She had finished her own, and poked her finger into the dough to show how it sprang right back again.

Finally everybody had a lump that would do the same thing. "Look what happens if we try to roll it out now," Mamma said. She pressed her dough down with a rolling pin. The ball wouldn't lie flat.

"It's young and tough," Mamma said. "We've got to tiptoe away and let it sleep," she said.

"When we come back, it will know how to behave." Someone laughed, thinking she was joking. But it was true. The dough had to rest.

To pass the time, Mamma led them down the hall to a dark room. A lantern-slide show was starting. It was all about children in many nations. The woman who ran the projector explained each picture.

When the show ended, Mamma took them back to the kitchen. The children were surprised to see that it was just as Mamma had said. The balls of dough were much softer now. Mamma showed them how to roll the dough out flat on the table.

"And now," Mamma said, "we're going to cut it up." With a little wheel, she sliced through her dough a dozen times, as fast as the blink of an eye. Mamma held the strips up for everybody to see. "Who knows what this is?" she said.

"Noodles!" everybody cried. Before long, the children were hanging their long noodles on racks to dry. Though the noodles still had to be cooked, it was hard not to sample some. Giggling children were running about with noodles hanging out of their mouths.

Just then, Cristina looked up and saw a tall woman in the doorway. Oh no! It was Mrs.

Palmer herself. Maybe she would think Mamma couldn't control her class.

But Mrs. Palmer smiled and even took a noodle that one of the children handed her. "Such enthusiasm and joy!" she said. "Who is in charge here?"

Mamma went right over, still wearing her apron and with her hands sticky with dough. Cristina put her hands over her eyes in embarrassment. Then she heard Mamma calling her name. She was going to introduce her to Mrs. Palmer!

Cristina wanted to hide. She tried to untie her apron with one hand and brush back her hair with the other. A little girl next to her laughed. "You've got flour in your hair," she said.

Cristina blushed wildly, and the apron flopped loose around her waist. She tried not to stare at Mrs. Palmer's diamond necklace.

"It's wonderful, what your mother is doing here," said Mrs. Palmer. Cristina nodded.

"Are you going to help her every day?"

"Just today. But when school is out, I want to come out and see everything at the fair."

"Everything?" Mrs. Palmer smiled. "It's a very big fair. Someone figured out that if you saw everything you'd have to walk at least 150 miles."

Cristina smiled shyly. "Well, I can try."

Mrs. Palmer turned to Cristina's mother. "I have a special job for a bright young girl. Many children from other nations are coming to the fair. I would like them to meet children from Chicago. Would you let Cristina be a guide to show some children through the fair?"

Cristina's heart leaped. Mamma said, "Would you like that, Cristina?"

"Oh, yes, Mamma," she said. "More than anything."

The two women laughed. "All right," said Mamma. "You can help Mrs. Palmer."

"When can you start?" Mrs. Palmer asked.

It was like a dream come true.

CHAPTER TWO

The White City

CRISTINA was nervous. She was about to start her first day as a guide. Earlier, she had walked around the fair with Papa and tried to read the huge book that described every exhibit. But it would have taken her all summer just to read the book!

She comforted herself with the thought that you really couldn't get lost at the fair. All you had to do was get aboard the little electric railroad that wound all through the grounds. It moved so fast—12 miles an hour!—that even after making stops at the larger buildings it took only twenty minutes for a complete trip.

Mrs. Palmer was waiting at the Children's

Pavilion when Cristina and Mamma arrived. Two girls about Cristina's age were standing with her. Cristina was relieved to see that they wore green school uniforms. She had worn her best dress, but worried that it might look shabby if she had to guide a princess.

The girls were from England. Their names were Alice and Nell, and they both carried little guidebooks. Cristina relaxed. They probably knew more about the fair than she did.

"We'd awfully like to see the Women's Building," Alice said. "The Queen has an exhibit there." Cristina supposed she meant the Queen of England.

Finding the Women's Building was easy, because it was right next to the Children's Pavilion. After walking through the beautiful white pillars in front, the girls found themselves in a huge hall. All around them were paintings and sculptures.

Alice read aloud from her guidebook. "Nothing in this building has been made by the hand of man. Everything here is the work of women."

"What about the building itself?" asked Nell. She and Alice looked at Cristina for an answer. Cristina bit her lip, for she wasn't sure.

Just then a woman standing nearby spoke up.

"I can answer that. My name is Sophia Hayden, and I am the architect who designed the Women's Building."

The girls from England were surprised. "But it's so large and magnificent! How could you have learned to do it?"

"I studied hard for four years in architect's school. But the fair was my first chance to design a building. People don't think women can do the same kinds of work that men do. We hope that the displays here will change their minds."

Alice and Nell giggled. "Our mothers don't work."

"That's too bad," said Sophia Hayden. "For they may have great talents to share with others." She pointed to the far end of the hall. "Walk down there and look at the mural on the wall. It was painted by Mary Cassatt, a great American artist."

They admired the mural. It showed three women and a girl picking fruit in an orchard. "It seems rather beautiful, really," said Alice. "We'll have something to tell our art teacher when we return. I don't think he knows there are any women artists."

Walking through the first floor, they found a medical exhibit. Nurses used life-size human models to show how to treat injuries and diseases. Some of the models were painted with blood or had broken limbs. The English girls hid their eyes and groaned. "I don't think I could bear nursing," said Alice.

But Cristina was fascinated. "What if you had to help someone in an emergency?" she said.

They moved upstairs, where they saw a group of Navajo women seated at a loom, weaving a blanket. It was bright red, with a design of black and brown.

"It's quite beautiful," Nell murmured.

"Thank you," replied a girl in a Navajo dress. "That's my mother working at the loom."

"Why, you speak English perfectly," said Nell.

"You do, too," the girl replied. Nell and Alice giggled.

Cristina introduced herself and the two English girls. "My name is Tahn-Moo-Whe," said the Navajo girl. She smiled when the girls tried to repeat her name. "Call me Sunbeam," she said.

Sunbeam showed them around the exhibit. It included shields, drums, jewelry, bead belts, baskets, and bows and arrows. "Navajo women made all these," said Sunbeam.

Nell examined one of the bows. "We practice

archery at our school in England," she said.

"Did you ever hunt animals with a bow and arrow?" asked Sunbeam.

Nell looked surprised. "Oh, no."

"I'll bet your English ancestors did," said Sunbeam.

"I guess that's true, isn't it?" Nell admitted.

"And the English had good weavers, too," said Sunbeam. She pointed out the way to the English exhibit. "Go over and see."

The first thing they saw in the English exhibit was a long cloth in a glass case. It was covered with colorful pictures that had been sewn with thread.

"This tapestry is a kind of history book," said Alice, reading from her guidebook. "The pictures tell the story of how William the Conquerer became King of England."

Cristina looked at the tapestry, following the story. William and his soldiers had crossed the sea on boats. In another picture, a comet appeared in the sky, causing people to be afraid. And then, there was a great battle. Lines of archers shot their arrows, and knights in armor charged forward on horses. Finally, William was crowned king. A little card on the glass case read, "Made by Matilda of Flanders around the year 1092."

"Wow. This tapestry is eight hundred years old!" said Cristina. "That was four centuries before Columbus arrived in America."

"I guess Sunbeam was right about English weavers," said Nell.

"Can you weave?" asked Cristina.

The girls shrugged. "It isn't necessary today. You can buy whatever you need."

Nearby, they found the Queen's own exhibit. It was a set of cloth table napkins. The card read, "Made from flax spun by Queen Victoria."

"Does this mean she wove the cloth herself?" asked Cristina. "Just like the Navajo women we saw?"

Nell seemed a little embarrassed. "Well, of course, but the Queen doesn't have to work," she said. "She has servants."

"I think it would be boring if you didn't have to do *some* work," Cristina said. "That's probably why she made the napkins."

As they continued the tour, they saw a lot more things that women were doing all over the world. The girls stopped in a hall where music composed by women was being played. They saw a whole library of books written by women.

Cristina spotted a model of a small village. "This is Kate Marsden's village," said Alice excitedly. "She heard about some lepers in Siberia who had no place to live. So she began to collect money to build a place for them. She spoke at our school, and all the girls donated something. And just to make sure the lepers would receive the money, Miss Marsden rode 7,000 miles on horseback to reach Siberia."

"*I'm* supposed to be *your* guide," laughed Cristina. "But you're telling me more about the fair than I know."

"Let's go outside and you can show us something," said Alice.

Luckily, the first thing they saw was a chocolate stand. Mrs. Palmer had given Cristina money to treat her guests, and they sat down with their cups of chocolate on the edge of the lagoon. Long boats with graceful curved ends were gliding back and forth on the water.

"Those are real gondolas made in Venice, Italy," said Cristina. "In Venice, you know, people use them to go around the city because they have canals instead of streets."

"Can we take a ride?" asked Alice.

"I was hoping you'd ask," said Cristina.

They chose a gondola with a red-and-green

striped awning over the seats in the middle. Two gondoliers, standing at either end of the boat, pushed the boat with long poles.

It was a wonderful way to see the fair. The lagoon wound all through it. Their boat passed under stone bridges that let people walk across the lagoon. The girls leaned back, ate their chocolate, and enjoyed the view.

Huge white domes and pillars stretched into the sky as far as they could see. "It truly is a White City, as people call it," said Alice. "All the buildings look like they're made of white marble."

"I'll tell you a secret," said Cristina. "It isn't really marble. The sides of the buildings are coated with plaster that has been painted white."

"How clever," said Alice.

The gondolier in front began to sing, and the other one took up the song. Cristina recognized it, and couldn't stop herself from singing, too. "Barchetta mia, Santa Lucia . . ."

"How did you know the words?" Alice asked when the song was finished.

"My mother's name is Lucia," Cristina explained, "and Papa likes to sing it for her. They came from Italy two years before I was born."

"Does Chicago have a great many Italians?"

"Yes. But there are Polish, Greeks, Irish, Russians, Germans . . . people from all over."

"I have always wondered something," said Alice. "I hope you won't mind my asking?"

"No, it's all right," said Cristina.

"How can you all get on together without fighting?"

Cristina laughed. "I guess it's because we're all Americans now," she said.

The gondoliers left them off at the Marine Cafe. It had ten towers with pointed roofs and porches where people could eat and admire the view. Alice and Nell were delighted to find that food of all nations was available here. "We must order an English tea," they said.

Cristina didn't like tea, but it turned out that an English "tea" included a lot of cookies, cakes, and toast with different kinds of jam. Cristina tried a little of everything.

"I really enjoyed that," she said when they were finished.

"It's the best meal of the day in England," said Alice.

The girls spent the rest of the afternoon wandering through the state buildings at the north end of the fair. Every state displayed its products from farms, factories, ranches—an overwhelming exhibit of everything the United States produced. "I'm exhausted," Alice finally admitted. "It seems as if America really is a series of countries, all of them different."

Cristina brought the girls back to Mrs. Palmer. "We had a perfectly wonderful time," Alice and Nell said, and Cristina beamed. "Give us your address, and we'll write," the English girls said.

Cristina went to meet Mamma at the Children's Pavilion. She found her with a group of teachers at the nursery that cared for infants. "Someone left a little baby girl here and hasn't come back for it," Mamma told her. "They think the baby may have been abandoned by a woman who has no husband."

They waited until the fair closed, but the mother did not appear. One of the teachers took the child home. As Cristina and her mother boarded the steam-engine railroad that went to their neighborhood, Cristina asked, "What will happen to the baby?"

"If the mother doesn't come back, it will go to an orphanage for children with no parents," Mamma said. She shook her head. "In those places, there are too many children and too few people to take care of them. But maybe Miss Addams will take the baby."

"Who is Miss Addams?" Cristina asked.

"Oh, a great woman. Very great. She has a house where anyone can come who needs help. And she loves children. You'll see her tomorrow. She is coming to the fair."

CHAPTER THREE

The Greatest Woman in Chicago

WHEN CRISTINA arrived the next day, she saw a crowd of boys and girls at the entrance to the Children's Pavilion. The children's faces were scrubbed and their hair neatly combed. The boys wore little jackets and ties and the girls wore neat, clean dresses. But they all looked as if they wanted to run wildly through the fair, gobbling chocolate and diving into the lagoon for a swim.

A tiny woman stepped forward and offered her hand. The woman's head bobbed to the side as she spoke. "You must be Cristina Ricci," she said. "I am Jane Addams. Mrs. Palmer said I could borrow you for the day."

"Are these all your children?" asked Cristina.

Miss Addams smiled. "Nobody else wants them. So I must be their mother, and their father, too."

Cristina saw that Miss Addams walked with a limp. "We can hire a rickshaw for you, ma'am," Cristina said. She pointed to a line of little wheeled carts with men standing ready to push them.

"And let someone roll me around as if I were sick? No indeed, thank you. All I need is someone to help me keep all my children together. I may not have two good legs, but I've used them all my life."

A little boy, about seven, began to tug at Miss Addams's skirt. "Midway," he said.

"I remember, Spiro," said Miss Addams. She pointed to Cristina. "By popular demand, our guide will lead us to the Midway." The children cheered.

The Midway was becoming the most popular part of the fair. The mile-long avenue held amazing sights and shows from all parts of the world. The first one they saw was an Irish castle. Over the archway was a sign reading "CEAD MILE FAILTE."

A little girl grasped Cristina's hand and

pointed to the words. "I know what that means. My Da was from Ireland. When his friends came to our house, he always said that. It means a hundred thousand welcomes."

Inside the castle, the children rushed up the steps to the tower. Miss Addams couldn't keep up. "Follow them," she told Cristina. "Keep them from falling off the roof."

Cristina thought she was joking, but when she reached the roof she saw them crowding between the gaps in the wall to see over the side. She pulled a couple of boys back by the seat of their pants, and the little Irish girl jumped forward into the gap.

When Cristina moved next to her, she saw an Irish village down below. Sheep grazed on the grass in front of little houses with straw roofs. Women were shearing the sheep and spinning the wool into cloth. A blacksmith hammered horseshoes in front of a blazing forge. "It looks just the way my Da told me his village looked," the Irish girl said.

She didn't want to go when the others were ready to leave. Miss Addams took the little girl's hand and said softly, "He's not there, Shannon."

Shannon looked up. "I know. He's in Heaven, with Mum."

"And they helped you find me," Miss Addams said.

They moved on down the Midway, taking a world tour in a few hours' time. They saw tents in which Bedouins lived in the Arabian desert. They looked into the crater of Kilauea, a Hawaiian volcano, and shivered inside an Eskimo igloo.

The others quickly left the igloo, but the boy named Spiro stayed behind. When Cristina went to get him, he pressed his hands against the wall. "You think this ice house is cold?" he asked Cristina.

"Don't you?" she said.

"Naw. It's nothing like sleeping in an alley in Chicago in February. These Eskimos are smart, see. Make a house out of ice and keep the wind from getting at you. Then you can stand the cold. I used some old boxes that people threw out."

"You slept in a box?" Cristina said. But Spiro had already run on, following the group into a Japanese bazaar. The children crowded around a counter where bright-colored paper toys were on sale. Miss Addams took out her purse and gave some pennies to each child. They rushed forward, picking up one toy and then another, trying to decide which they liked best.

"Most of these children have never had any toys," Miss Addams said to Cristina. "I wish I could give them more."

Cristina used her guide's pass to admit them inside Hagenbeck's Animal Show. A thousand parrots lined the entranceway, all talking at once so that no one could understand what they said. Inside the arena, they watched lions riding horses and a tiger pedaling a tricycle. "I wouldn't believe it even if I did see it," Spiro said to Cristina.

Finally they came to the fair's most popular attraction—the giant Ferris Wheel right in the center of the Midway. The whole group fit easily inside one of the cars. Each of the 36 cars on the Wheel could hold 60 people. They sat on plush-covered chairs softer than the sofa in Cristina's home. The children soon found that each chair swiveled around in a circle. By the time their car reached the top of the Wheel, some of them were too dizzy to look out the glass windows.

But Cristina jumped up to stare at the view. She could see the whole fair at once, and beyond it the vast city of Chicago. Miss Addams came to stand beside her at the window. "It's so big!" said Cristina. "I never saw the city like this before."

"Yes, and just think," said Miss Addams, "only

22 years ago, a great fire almost destroyed the entire city. But Chicago refused to die. Its people built it up again. They can do anything they set their minds to. Now I have to make them think about children like mine."

After the trip on the Ferris Wheel, everybody was hungry. They found a restaurant with a sign that declared: "Home Cooking." Inside, the children's eyes bugged out as they saw the food on display: turkeys roasting on spits, whole hams glazed with honey, ears of corn, onion-stuffed tomatoes, baked apples—every kind of food that came from American farms.

The children were up to the challenge. They ate for nearly an hour, taking their plates back for more time and time again. Cristina liked to eat, but she had never seen anybody put away food like Miss Addams's children. It seemed to her that Shannon, the little Irish girl, ate more than she weighed before she entered the restaurant.

"This is going to cost you a lot," Cristina said to Miss Addams.

"Mrs. Palmer is paying for the children's outing," said Miss Addams. "It's hard for them to turn down food. Some of these children have worked in factories for twelve hours a day, with only one meal. When I found Shannon, she was

searching through garbage cans in back of a restaurant. Let them come in the front door for once."

Cristina told Miss Addams about the English girls she had met yesterday. "Their parents are wealthy," she said. "They'll never have to work in their lives. It doesn't seem fair."

"It isn't," said Miss Addams firmly. "That is why I have devoted my life to helping children who have no one else. But I can take in only a few, and there are so many others, and not only in Chicago."

Leaving the restaurant, they crossed one of the bridges over the lagoon. The children stopped to look at the view. All around them stood the wonderful buildings of white painted stone.

"It's really like a fairy-tale city," said Cristina.

"Just think that it was built in a little more than a year," replied Miss Addams. "It shows what people can do when they are determined. What if Chicago decided to use its wealth and energy to build houses and apartments for the homeless? Wouldn't that be a greater project than the fair?"

"The children really are enjoying themselves," Cristina pointed out.

"They are, for one day. But did you know that

these buildings will all be destroyed when the fair is over?"

Cristina was surprised. "No, I didn't."

"It's just a dream of what a city could be like. We mustn't let that dream fade away. I for one will not be satisfied until all of Chicago lives up to the promise of the fair."

They finished the afternoon with a visit to the Fisheries Building. Cristina gaped along with the others at the tanks of strange tropical fish. "Look at this monster," cried Spiro. Everyone joined him in front of a tank where a huge shark swam alone. It spotted them and bared its rows of jagged teeth. With a flick of its tail, the shark swam forward until it bumped against the glass. Everyone took a step backward.

"It's perfectly safe," said an attendant. "The glass is an inch and a half thick."

"Yeah?" said Spiro. He cautiously tapped the glass, pulling his hand back as the shark lunged for it. "I wonder who gets to feed this fish."

"Maybe they'll give you the job," said one of the other boys. "Show us how you can swim, Spiro."

They laughed and moved on. Little Shannon stayed behind, staring at the shark. When Cristina took her hand, the girl looked up. "I wonder if it gets lonely in there all by itself," she said.

As the children lined up to board the railway home, each of them shook Cristina's hand. Shannon was the last one. "I had a good time," she said. Her eyes sparkled. "Thank you."

Cristina slowly walked back to the Children's Pavilion, thinking about Miss Addams's children. She saw the fair with new eyes. Next year it would all be gone. Would it once again become just a swamp next to Lake Michigan? What was the point of building it?

Cristina thought of the look in little Shannon's eyes. Would all the wonderful inventions on display at the fair do anything to help her?

"So, Cristina," said a familiar voice, "I hear you've spent the day with the greatest woman in Chicago." It was Mrs. Palmer.

Cristina was startled. "Most people say that you are the greatest."

Mrs. Palmer laughed and shook her head. "I don't have the courage to do what Jane Addams does. Did you notice that she has trouble walking? As a young woman, she had a spinal illness. The doctors said she would never walk again. She proved them wrong, and then decided to devote her life to the less fortunate. With her own money, she bought the old Hull house. It was one of the few buildings that survived the great fire. She opens her doors to anyone who has no place to live."

"Some of the children told me about their lives," said Cristina. "I didn't realize . . ."

"Truly sad, I know. I hope they enjoyed themselves at the fair."

"Oh, they loved it," said Cristina. "But . . ." She hesitated. "Miss Addams said it is only a promise of what Chicago should be like. I think she feels that . . . the money could have been spent better."

Mrs. Palmer frowned. "Well," she said, "the fair will bring millions of people to Chicago. They will spend money here, and that will help everyone. Many people found work building the fair. And we're showing the whole world what a great city we live in."

Cristina didn't want to argue with Mrs. Palmer. But she asked, "Do you think that some of the money people spend at the fair could go to Miss Addams?"

"I have donated money to her charity. But she won't take too much from wealthy people. She thinks we'll start telling her how to run her settlement house." Mrs. Palmer smiled. "She's probably right."

"But couldn't something be done to help her?"

Mrs. Palmer looked at Cristina. "You'd really like to, wouldn't you? Well, let me think about it. Perhaps we can find a way."

CHAPTER FOUR

The Ruby Princess

CRISTINA finally got to meet a princess—from India. Bitya was the daughter of a Maharajah. But she caused more trouble than anyone else Cristina showed around the fair that summer.

Mrs. Palmer took Cristina aside and said, "Our little princess is used to doing anything she wants. Her father sent a chaperone to watch over her. But I think you will have your hands full today."

She was right. Cristina suggested that they look at some of the beautiful jewelry that the women of India made. But after a glance, Bitya said, "I've seen all this before. Show me something new."

They went to the Horticultural Building, where flowers and farm products were on display. California had sent a whole elephant made out of walnuts. On the elephant's back was a howdah, or a box with a seat inside, decorated with oranges and lemons. Bitya laughed when she saw it. "How interesting! But I have ridden on a real elephant."

Bitya pointed to a sign. "The Crystal Cave! I have to see it. Let's go inside."

Bitya's chaperone, an older woman named Marani, seemed nervous inside the cave. It wasn't really that dark, for crystals on the ceiling and walls reflected electric lights at either end. Bitya whispered to Cristina, "Take us someplace that will really frighten Marani."

Cristina suggested the Ferris Wheel, for she thought that would seem dangerous enough for Bitya. But before they got there, Bitya spotted a new feature of the Midway. It was a hot-air balloon ride, the only thing at the fair that went higher than the Ferris Wheel. "Marani will never go on that," Bitya said. "So you must take me."

Marani was indeed horrified. At first she flatly refused to let Bitya go on the ride. But the man who operated the balloon showed her the strong rope connected to it. "It's a captive balloon, ma'am," he said. "Can't get loose." Marani reluctantly gave permission, and Bitya and Cristina climbed inside the wicker basket.

Up and up they went, past the top of the Ferris Wheel, until the people on the ground below seemed like ants. Bitya rushed around the basket, shrieking with delight. Cristina peeped over the side. She could see sailboats far out on Lake Michigan. A flock of gulls flew below the balloon. The White City shimmered in the sun beneath her feet. It was beautiful, but she couldn't enjoy it. She tried not to think about falling.

"Oh, don't you wish we could just float on over the whole city?" said Bitya. "Fly like the birds and go wherever the wind takes us?"

Cristina gulped. "I guess so."

Suddenly, Bitya reached into her sari. She pulled out a little dagger with a jeweled handle. "My father gave me this for protection," she said. "Why don't I cut the rope with it?"

"No!" Cristina shouted. She wasn't sure that the dagger could cut through the thick rope, but Bitya seemed ready to try.

Bitya frowned. "Why not? I thought Americans were daring people. What's the matter with you?"

"Please. Sit down," said Cristina.

Bitya shrugged and put her dagger away. But she kept peering over the sides of the basket as the man pulled them back to the ground.

After that, Bitya wanted to try anything that moved fast. They took an electric motorboat along the lagoon, for gondolas were too slow for Bitya. Then they rode the Ice Railway, which was a long slide covered entirely with ice. Even Marani could not resist taking the ride, but Cristina saw that she kept her eyes closed the whole time.

"How do they make so much ice and keep it from melting?" said Bitya. "When we want ice at home, we have to bring it from the mountains."

"Under the ice," said Cristina, "there are copper tubes filled with some kind of very cold gas. It's a new invention called refrigeration."

"Amazing!" said Bitya. "I will have father buy one of these for me."

"I think you need electricity to make it work," Cristina said.

"Do they sell it here in Chicago? I'll bring some home."

Cristina shook her head. "I wish Papa were here to explain it. He works for the electric company."

"Does he? You must be very rich."

"No, no, not at all."

"I thought all Americans were rich."

"I wish you had been with me a few weeks ago," Cristina said. "You would have met some children who slept in alleys and had to beg in the streets."

"In America? How could that be? Does your president know about this?"

"I don't know," said Cristina. "But I'll bet that Jane Addams will tell him."

"Who is she?"

"A woman I met who gives poor children a place to live. She brought some of them to the fair. You should have seen their faces when she gave them some money for toys. People call her the greatest woman in Chicago, because she uses her own money to help others."

Bitya clapped her hands. "How wonderful that someone would do this," she said.

"But she needs more money," said Cristina without thinking.

Bitya winked and nodded. When Marani stopped to buy doughnuts from a vendor, Bitya pulled Cristina behind a pillar. Bitya removed her earrings and gave them to Cristina. "Here," she whispered. "These are rubies. Give them to Miss Addams. She can sell them."

"Oh, I couldn't," Cristina protested.

Bitya slipped the earrings into Cristina's purse. "You must take them. I will be most insulted if you do not."

As they ate the doughnuts, Cristina worried about the earrings. But Bitya seemed to have forgotten about them already. She asked Cristina, "Why do they make a hole in the middle of these little cakes? It seems a cheat, for they are so delicious you want more."

"I don't know. That's just the way they are."

Bitya pointed to one of the most beautiful buildings on the lagoon. It had an immense entrance with five golden arches covered with decorations. "This looks like an Indian temple," Bitya said.

"It's the Transportation Building."

"Transportation? More things that go fast? Show me."

Inside, Bitya was disappointed to find that most of the exhibits were huge locomotives. They didn't move, though you could sit inside them. Then she saw a sign that said, "Elevator rides, 10 cents."

The elevator took them to the top of the building's tower. Cristina had ridden it before, but still didn't like being shut up in the little room. Marani put her arms around Bitya when she felt the elevator move, but Bitya said, "It's all right. Just some more magic American electricity."

At the top of the building, they could see all the way to the lake. A big crowd had gathered there. "Today is the day that Columbus's ships are arriving from Spain," Cristina told Bitya. "Let's walk to the lakefront."

Bitya didn't like walking, so she hired rickshaws to carry them. Spain had sent to the fair three full-size models of Columbus's ships, the *Nina,* the *Pinta,* and the *Santa Maria.* They sailed across the Atlantic, just as Columbus had 401 years before.

But amazingly, the same day the Spanish ships arrived at the fair, so did a Viking ship from Norway. It was shaped like a sea serpent, with a head and tail. Round shields hung along its sides.

People in the crowd were arguing. "What is all the fuss?" Bitya asked.

"Well," Cristina said. "The sailors from Norway say that one of their ancestors, a Viking called Leif Ericson, actually arrived in America long before Columbus did."

"I never heard that story," Bitya said.

"The newspapers here have had articles about it," Cristina explained.

Cristina spotted someone she knew staring at the ships. It was Sunbeam, the Navajo girl she had met at the Women's Building. Cristina waved, and Sunbeam walked over. Cristina introduced her to Bitya.

"You're really from India?" said Sunbeam. "Then you are the first Indian I've ever met." Sunbeam smiled. "Even though that's what people call us."

"I know the story," said Bitya. "Columbus thought he had arrived at the islands named the Indies, so he called the people Indians."

"But even after they found out the truth, we remained Indians."

"It truly is unfair," said Bitya. "What is *your* name for your people?"

"Navajo."

Bitya hugged Sunbeam. "I will tell everybody in India that the real Americans are Navajos."

"And don't forget." Sunbeam pointed to the ships. "We were here before Columbus *or* Leif Ericson," she said.

"Of course," Bitya said.

When Bitya found out that Sunbeam's mother

had an exhibit, she insisted on seeing it. She invited Sunbeam to share her rickshaw on the ride to the Women's Building.

While they were admiring the weaving, Mrs. Palmer came up. "I see our princess has made a friend," she said to Cristina.

Cristina looked over her shoulder and saw that Bitya was chatting with Sunbeam. "Yes, but I've got something I have to ask you about," Cristina said. She slipped from her purse the ruby earrings that Bitya had given her.

When she explained what happened, Mrs. Palmer said, "You were right to tell me. I don't think her parents know how generous she is." She took the earrings and said, "I'll return these to her father, the Maharajah. But I think we can count on him for a donation to Miss Addams— as a reward for your honesty. Besides, I have a plan to help her. And this time I don't think she'll turn us down."

CHAPTER FIVE

Chicago Day

BY THE TIME school started in September, Cristina thought she had seen everything at the fair. It had been a wonderful experience. When she told her classmates about her summer job, they agreed that she must be the luckiest kid in Chicago.

But that wasn't the end of her adventure. October 9 was Chicago Day at the fair. This was the anniversary of the Great Fire of 1871, when two-thirds of the city burned to the ground. Admission to the fair was free that day, and all the schools had a holiday.

Mamma was busier than ever, for she had become famous for her children's cooking classes.

Some of Mrs. Palmer's wealthy friends came to watch. And after one of them tasted Mamma's lasagna, she offered to lend Mamma money to start a restaurant when the fair was over.

"Mamma, are you going to do it?" Cristina said when she heard the news.

Mamma shook her head. "I don't know. I like to cook for my family and friends. But who knows what strangers will like? I don't want to go into debt. It's too much of a risk. We could lose everything we've saved from Papa's job."

Papa nudged Cristina. "We'll talk her into it. I'll put in electric lights and I bet Mamma Ricci's will be the best restaurant in Chicago."

Mamma blushed. "Oh, no. Just call it Ricci's."

"Mamma Ricci's," said Papa firmly. "That way, everybody will know whose cooking is best."

On Chicago Day, Papa took Cristina on his own tour of the fair. They went to the Electricity Building, where the Edison Company had an exhibit. He showed her the huge generators that made electricity. She felt the thrum-thrum-thrum as the big wheels went around so fast that she couldn't see them.

"And see what electricity makes," Papa said. They went into the Egyptian temple, where spooky lights shone behind frosted glass. Cristina could see the ancient carvings on the walls.

"No place will ever be dark again," said Papa. "Pretty soon, every house will have its own electric lights. But that's not all electricity can do." He showed her the model home where machines did all the work. Machines to clean the rugs, to wash windows—even one to knead dough!

"Mamma will never use one of those," Cristina said. "You can tell the difference between the dough she makes and anyone else's. She says her fingers know when it's ready."

"Maybe so," admitted Papa. "But here's something I know she'll like."

"Oh, yes," Cristina said when she saw it. "Whenever I took children in here, they spent a long time looking at this." It was the kinetoscope invented by Thomas Edison. You looked through a little window in a box and saw pictures that moved just like they were real. Some people had tried to pry open the back of the box, thinking that there must be puppets inside.

"Did you hear Edison's phonograph play the sound of people's voices?" Papa asked. "You know what I think? You could put that together with the kinetoscope to make a machine that showed talking pictures. And someday . . . put one of those machines in every house."

Cristina shook her head. "Papa, what a dream!

If there was such a machine, nobody would want to do anything but watch those pictures."

"Ah, you wait and see, Cristina. Only seven years till the twentieth century begins. This fair only gives an idea of what the future will be like. You'll live long enough to see a lot of things more amazing than that."

They went outside and boarded the electric railway. It took them all around the fair. "This is much better than a steam-engine train," Papa said. "It doesn't make any noise or smoke. You don't need anything but an electric battery. Turn a switch and off it goes. And you know what? Somebody has already hooked up a battery to a carriage. Someday people will ride around in those." He clapped his hands. "No more horses."

"Oh, no, Papa," said Cristina. "I can't imagine Chicago without horses."

He smiled. "You'll see," he said. "Someday, someday."

As they rode along, Cristina looked at the crowds of people walking through the White City. More than 700,000 people came through the gates that day—half the population of Chicago. Cristina thought about Miss Addams's hope that Chicago would live up to the fair's promise. If Papa's dreams could come true, why not Miss Addams's dream too?

Maybe . . . if Papa was right, all these electric inventions would change everything. People wouldn't have to work so hard. Machines would do the work. And everybody would be as rich as Mrs. Palmer.

Well, maybe not that rich. But still, they could have houses of their own. Children wouldn't have to sleep in alleys. But carriages without horses? What would become of the horses?

That day, the fair was open till midnight. When Mamma got off work, the Ricci family ate dinner at one of the many crowded restaurants at the fair. Mamma frowned over her plate. "This is not really such good food," she said. "And look at all the people who pay money for it."

Papa winked across the table at Cristina. Both of them knew what Mamma was thinking: maybe a restaurant wasn't such a crazy idea.

After dark, the great plazas of the fair filled with people waiting for the big fireworks display. As the rockets exploded in the sky, everybody cheered. It was Chicago's proudest day. Its people had recovered from the Great Fire and built a fair that the whole world had come to see.

Cristina loved to watch the fireworks, but when they were finished, she turned to look at the White City at night. All the windows of the buildings sparkled like jewels in the darkness. She closed her eyes and imagined what Chicago would look like if every house had electric lights. It would be a great diamond necklace curving around the lake.

That evening, Mrs. Palmer had invited the Riccis to an awards ceremony in the Administration Building. Spotlights lit up the big gold dome as they went inside. Cristina was excited to see Miss Addams sitting on the speakers' stand.

But there were so many speeches that Cristina nearly fell asleep. Finally Mrs. Palmer stood up and thanked the people who had helped to make the fair a success. She named all the women who had served in the Children's Pavilion. Cristina clapped loudly when Mamma's name was read.

"It is a shame that the buildings at the fair will have to be pulled down," said Mrs. Palmer. "But to maintain them would be too costly. However, we are glad to announce that the fairgrounds will be turned into a park. Trees, grass, and flowers will be planted along the lakefront.

Every family in Chicago can bring their children here to enjoy the beauties of nature."

Then Mrs. Palmer said that the Board of Women's Managers had received a donation from an Indian Maharajah. Cristina smiled to herself. "We have set up a fund especially for the care and education of needy young people," said Mrs. Palmer. "And we are appointing Jane Addams to be in charge of using the money."

The audience stood and applauded as Miss Addams came forward. "This is a wonderful way to carry on the memory of the fair," she said. "The White City allowed us to dream. None of us should be satisfied until Chicago has turned the dream into reality. We must always remember that our children are the future."

When Miss Addams finished, Mrs. Palmer said, "I should add that a young Chicagoan gave me the idea of creating a children's fund." She looked out at the crowd.

Oh no! thought Cristina. "There she is," said Mrs. Palmer. "Please give a hand for a very hard-working guide, Cristina Ricci."

Papa pushed her to her feet as the crowd applauded. Cristina blushed with pride.

After the ceremony, Miss Addams met Cristina and her parents. "I want to thank you," said Miss

Addams. "This money will mean a lot to my children."

"I really didn't do anything," Cristina said.

"You cared," said Jane Addams. "I saw it when you showed the children around the fair that day. Your parents should be proud of raising such a fine daughter."

Mamma and Papa beamed. "We are."

At last they boarded the train to go home. The steam engine pulled it along the tracks high above the streets. Cristina looked down at the gas lanterns on each street corner. They were so dim compared to the electric lights at the fair. She was sure Papa was right. Someday Chicago would look like the White City.

Cristina would never forget this summer. She had learned a lot about other people. She had seen enough wonderful things to last a lifetime. Most importantly, she had found out what she wanted to do with her life. One day, she decided, she would work with Miss Addams to make her dream of Chicago come true.

MAKING
NOODLES

THOUGH WE usually think of noodles as an Italian dish, they really come from China. In the year 1270, Marco Polo, a native of Venice, Italy, went to China with his father and uncle. Marco spent 25 years there before returning home. He wrote a book about his travels. Some people thought the stories he told were so amazing that they must be made up.

But when Marco told how Chinese made

noodles from flat, soft dough, he changed Italian cooking. Italians soon began to cut the dough into many kinds of strips and shapes. The Italians called this food *pasta,* which means "dough." It has become a worldwide favorite.

Even the tomato sauce that many people serve with spaghetti or noodles did not come from Italy. Europeans did not know about the tomato until Christopher Columbus, another Italian, made his journeys to America. The Native Americans had been growing tomatoes for centuries. When Columbus brought it back to Europe, it became an important part of Italian cooking.

Materials Needed

Flour, Egg, Rolling pin, Cutting wheel, Pot to boil water, Colander.

Steps

You can make noodles just the way Mamma Ricci did in the story. Start with a small amount, and you can gradually use more ingredients to make a lot of pasta.

1. Measure ¾ cup of flour and place it on a smooth surface.

2. Make a little mound with a hollow well in the middle.

3. Break an egg—carefully—and discard the shell.

4. Mix the egg white and yolk into the flour. You can use your fingers or a fork.

5. Knead the flour. Press it down with your palms. Push your thumbs into it to build up a ball. Press it down again. Keep this up until the ball looks smooth and silky. If the dough starts to stick to the table, sprinkle a little flour on the

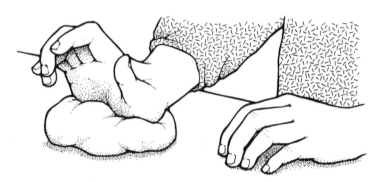

table. If you get tired, you can rest. The dough will wait.

6. Wrap the dough in wax paper or plastic wrap and let it rest for 20 or 30 minutes. Do not put it in the refrigerator.

7. Sprinkle a little more flour on the table. Rub your rolling pin with flour, too. Roll the dough as thin as you can. As the dough spreads out, roll from the center outward to the edges. You may have to spread some more flour on the table or rolling pin from time to time.

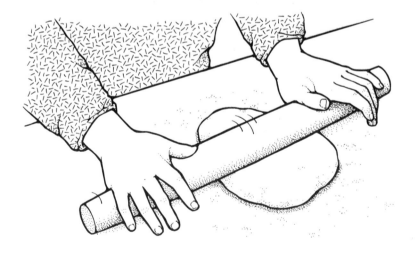

8. Cut the dough into strips. Have a place ready to hang the strips till you have cut them all.

9. Drop the strips into boiling water. They will

cook much faster than packaged dry pasta. Leave them in the water only about three minutes. Then pour the noodles into a colander in the sink so the water can drain out. Enjoy!

Tips

1. Because uncooked eggs can contain bacteria, you really shouldn't eat the noodles until they are cooked.

2. If you don't want to boil the noodles right away, dry the strips for about ten minutes. Then wrap them in wax paper or plastic wrap and put them in the refrigerator. They will keep for a day.

3. If you make a hole in the dough while rolling it, you can patch it with another piece and roll it down.

4. The amount of pasta in the recipe should be enough for two people. You can double the ingredients (1-½ cups flour; two eggs), or triple them. But more than that will be difficult to knead and roll flat.

5. As you get better, you can try making some of the many pasta shapes. You can make stars, circles, or little bow ties. You could cut squares of pasta for ravioli. Put a teaspoonful of cooked spinach or meat on one square, and then press

a second square on top. Moisten the edges with water so they will stick together.

6. Spaghetti, macaroni, ziti, and other tube-shaped pasta are usually made with a machine. But old-time Italian cooks could make tubes by wrapping pasta dough around knitting needles. It's hard to do, but the pasta still tastes good, even if it's messy.

7. There are lots of canned sauces to spread over pasta. But eating fresh pasta with just a little butter or magarine, and maybe some grated cheese, is delicious, too.